MARITIME MONSTERS

A FIELD GUIDE

STEVE VERNON
ILLUSTRATIONS BY JEFF SOLWAY

NIMBUS PUBLISHING

OLD HOOK-SNOUT (PRINCE EDWARD ISLAND)

It was August 1883—a day so dry the trees were hoping for hound dogs. Young Billy Walker decided to go fishing. He aimed to catch a big one.

"I got big-fish bait," Billy said to his buddy, Caleb Myers. "My mom's roast beef."

"You'll catch something swift and sudden for stealing Sunday supper," Caleb predicted.

"Not so bad as what you'll catch," Billy said, "since we're taking your dad's dory."

"Why do we need a dory?" Caleb asked.

"The bigger the boat, the bigger the fish," Billy said. "I mean to catch a big one."

"Maybe we need a bigger boat," Caleb said. "That's an awful lot of roast beef."

"It won't be after we eat some," Billy replied.

The boys rowed the dory out into the middle of the lake. They both carefully checked their fishing lines, spat on their hooks for luck, and spread the roast beef around.

"The stink of that old beef will bring the fish a-running," Billy said.

"Fish don't run," Caleb said. "They got no feet."

"Well, something's coming at us," Billy said.

The two boys smelled a reek worse than feeted-up rubber boots. The water churned around the dory like boiling water when it's ready for the noodles. Old Hook-Snout roared out of the deep water, huge and high and one-eyed, with a nose like a giant fish hook.

"Row for it!" Billy shouted.

Caleb didn't bother rowing. He dove into the water and swam, faster than you can say "wet." Billy jumped in after him as Old Hook-Snout belly-flopped onto the dory with all of his weight, smashing the little boat into toothpick splinters.

"He swam down into a whirlpool," Billy told his dad.

"I could see the ocean at the end of the whirlpool," Caleb added.

"You're grounded," the boys' parents said. "For sinking a dory and hijacking a roast beef. No more fishing for you."

Wet as they were, "ground" sounded simply grand to Billy and Caleb.

LOCATION: About thirty kilometres east of Charlottetown, Prince Edward Island—close to the town of Avondale, deep in the waters of O'Keefe's Lake

DIET: Dories, fishermen, and the occasional old rubber boot

SIZE: Old Hook-Snout is about twenty feet long and weighs five thousand pounds.

DESCRIPTION: A huge, weird-looking creature, Old Hook-Snout has a sail-sized fin nearly five feet high. He is covered in shiny scales that gleam like silver dollars fished out of a pirate's sunken treasure chest. His head is as round as a giant guppy bowl and he has a single bloodshot eyeball—not to mention his gnarly beak of a nose that looks like a giant, twisted fish hook.

FREQUENCY OF SIGHTINGS: Hard to find, but maybe he's just shy. Still, Old Hook-Snout has been known to swim a long way for the smell of roast beef, so be careful where you scatter your leftover sandwiches—or better yet, stick to ham, cheese, and ketchup.

SPECIAL MONSTER-HUNTING ADVICE: Wear your sunglasses—those silver scales are awfully bright—and bring along a clothespin for your nose. You'd smell funny, too, if you had a hook for a nose.

THE CROUSETOWN CANARY (NOVA SCOTIA)

Mr. Mokey is a big, noble cat. His owner calls him Moose-Butt although his real name is Muhrroww-Burrupp, just the same as his daddy-cat.

Mr. Mokey doesn't have much use for humans. Humans are dumb. They always work through naptime and petting time. The only thing humans are good for is ear-skritching and opening cans.

The day before yesterday, Mr. Mokey watched a human hang her damp fur on a rope in her backyard. Mr. Mokey couldn't imagine why she'd ever let her fur get wet in the first place. Didn't she know how to lick herself clean?

That's when that big old bird swooped down and nearly caught her in mid-fur-hang, just as Mr. Mokey had caught those feathered chew toys at his neighbour's birdseed box the day before yesterday.

Mmmmmm, Mr. Mokey thought.

Only this human-chasing bird wasn't an ordinary bird. We're talking B-I-R-D, a word that Mr. Mokey could spell just as easily as V-E-T. That B-I-R-D was at least two tomcats and a kitten long, and nearly three tomcats wide. It was garbage-bag black and smelled like old, stale cat food.

Mmmmmm, Mr. Mokey thought.

The next morning Mr. Mokey waited on the sidewalk, not moving, not making a sound, pretending he was fast asleep. Even when those little feathered chew toys came over to tweet and flutter at the birdseed box, Mr. Mokey didn't move.

Mr. Mokey was waiting for the B-I-R-D.

Then all at once Mr. Mokey's shadow was swallowed by a larger shadow, as black as the footprints of midnight, gliding across the ground. He heard wings beating loudly. To Mr. Mokey those wings sounded like dog barks, big and loud and getting closer with every beat. Mr. Mokey would have caught that big old B-I-R-D if he hadn't accidentally run in the other direction.

Brrrrrr, Mr. Mokey thought.

Today Mr. Mokey decided to surprise that B-I-R-D by hiding behind the big square that let sunlight into the living room.

Purrrrrrr, Mr. Mokey thought.

LOCATION: Crousetown, Nova Scotia—about twenty kilometres southwest of Lunenburg and fifteen kilometres south of Bridgewater

DIET: Bird feeders, sacks of seed, and any house cat or housewife who isn't quick enough to get away

SIZE: The Crousetown Canary is two feet high and two and a half feet long with a five-foot wingspan, and weighs in at approximately ten pounds. As monsters go that's pretty puny, but it's awfully big for a bird.

DESCRIPTION: It's a great feathered bird as black as the shadow of midnight.

FREQUENCY OF SIGHTINGS: Seen several times around Crousetown in the summer of 2008.

SPECIAL MONSTER-HUNTING ADVICE: A fishnet might be a good idea, but leave the butterfly net at home. If you are lucky enough to catch that big old bird, save a drumstick for the cat.

THE NOT-SO-CUDDLY KRAKEN (NEWFOUNDLAND)

On October 26, 1873, a pair of old fishermen named Angus and Walter spotted a dark shape drifting a few metres away from their dory in the waters of Conception Bay.

"Sea trash," Angus said. "There's a ship wrecked, sure as gumboots. That bit of flotsam floating there might be worth something if we fish it out."

Walter wasn't so sure.

"That doesn't look like any flotsam I've ever seen," he said.

"Since when have your eyes been good for anything more than keeping your nostrils away from your hairline?" Angus asked. "That's flotsam for sure."

While the two were arguing, the shape shot forward, rearing up out of the water.

"Cuttlefish!" Angus shouted.

"Kraken," Walter corrected.

They were both right. "Cuttlefish" and "kraken" are names given to giant squid (*architeuthis dux* or Archie-two-this-ducks to you scientific types)—over forty feet of arms and appetite, and longer than a school bus.

Don't mess with a Newfoundlander and his boat.

Quick as you could say "cut," Angus snatched up a hatchet and hacked off a squid arm. Walter slashed at a tentacle with his fish knife and kicked the creature square in the eyeball. It made a mushy sound, like he'd jumped foot-first into a giant gumboot full of lasagne.

Nothing helped. The squid was going to eat that dory, fishermen and all.

"We're done for!" Angus shouted.

"Not hardly," Walter said, plunging his hands into the water toward the squid. He wiggled his fingers and the squid let go of the dory.

"What in the name of Neptune's mildewed swim shorts did you just do?" Angus asked.

"I tickled his armpits," Walter answered, sniffing at his fingers, "and he needs a case or two of industrial-strength deodorant."

"You do too," Angus said with an even bigger sniff. "Nothing sticks to your fingers worse than squid gunk. Peeeee-cod-liver-oil-eewwwwww."

LOCATION: Spotted at various locations off the Grand Banks of Newfoundland, in waters that can reach from 90 to 4,500 metres deep

DIET: Fish, whale, and more fish—with the occasional fisherman thrown in for flavour

SIZE: The size and weight can vary depending on the age of the squid; the squid that was spotted in Conception Bay was estimated to be about ten feet long and over a hundred pounds. However, there are records of squid that had grown to about forty-three feet and nearly six hundred pounds.

DESCRIPTION: These squid have eight arms, two long tentacles, a mouthful of teeth, and a thousand suction-cup suckers, as sticky as lollipops.

FREQUENCY OF SIGHTINGS: They're seen fairly often by deepwater fishermen all across the world.

SPECIAL MONSTER-HUNTING ADVICE: Find your self a good recipe for deep-fried squid. A twenty-foot-long squid is an awful lot of calamari.

GOUGOU OF CHALEUR BAY (NEW BRUNSWICK)

It was the year 1612. On a moonless night off Miscou Island, in the mouth of Chaleur Bay, a sailing ship waited for daylight to come so the cod that filled the Orphan Banks could be harvested. Young François, the youngest and smallest sailor on the ship, stood at the railing, picking bits of the beef he'd eaten for dinner from his teeth with a twig. Toothbrushes were hard to find back then. François shivered in the evening cold.

"Are you frightened?" a gravelly voice said from behind François.

François sighed. It was Jean-Claude, the biggest of the sailors and a bully besides.

"You should be scared," Jean-Claude said, "for off of this island prowls the Gougou."

"That's just a story," François said.

"A story is a cloak truth hides behind," Jean-Claude replied. "Gougou slops around Chaleur Bay in big old gumboots, slipping sailors into her sack and saving them for midnight snacks."

François stared up through the tangled maze of mast, line, and sail above his head. The stars peeked out of the darkness like bright, hungry eyes.

"Ha!" Jean-Claude laughed nastily and pushed François down. "You little baby. You're scared of a bit of darkness."

Just then a shape rose out of the dark waters. Gougou stood over the ship, her long, seaweed-green hair tangled around her dark eyes and her large, hungry mouth with a long shawl of tattered sailcloth about her shoulders and head. She plucked Jean-Claude up and dropped him into the leather lunch bag that hung at her hip.

She smiled at François. Her teeth were gnarled and nasty. François saw a little something caught between two of them. Without thinking, he offered Gougou his little twig toothpick.

Gougou laughed, a grating harsh *haw-haw-haw* that sounded like ice breaking against rocks. She reached down. For an instant François worried she'd grab him for dessert. But instead, Gougou snapped a piece off the mizzen-mast, jammed it between her teeth, and splashed off into the darkness of Chaleur Bay.

"Enjoy your bully beef," François said.

Even monsters need to keep their teeth clean.

LOCATION: Gougou is believed to live in a dark cave on the island of Miscou, north of New Brunswick.

DIET: Seals and sea fish and sailors

SIZE: At least fifty feet tall, though Gougou is usually seen wading through Chaleur Bay, so no one knows exactly how big she is.

DESCRIPTION: Gougou looks like a giant, ancient, green sea-woman. She wears a shawl made out of sailcloth, which makes it hard to see her face unless she's grinning at you, or getting set to chew you up.

FREQUENCY OF SIGHTINGS: Gougou was originally reported back in the early 1600s by Samuel de Champlain; however, the Maliseet and Mi'kmaq have been telling tales about old Gougou since back before calendars came into fashion.

SPECIAL MONSTER-HUNTING ADVICE: Personally, I'd advise getting away from her—fast. Maybe in a speedboat or on a rocket ship, if you happen to have one handy. Gougou has an awfully long reach.

OLD NED
(NEW BRUNSWICK)

Jean-Paul drove the spike deep into the heart of the freshly felled pine tree. The spike was attached to a length of solid iron chain and three carefully sharpened hooks—each the size of a small anchor.

"I guess that log won't go anywhere now that you've nailed it down," Andre wisecracked.

"This isn't a log," Jean-Paul said, as he smeared the hooks with salt cod and pickled pork. "This is a fishing lure."

"You're figuring on fishing with salt cod and pork scraps?" Andre asked.

"I'm fishing for Old Ned, the lake monster," Jean-Paul replied.

"Old Ned?" Andre asked. "Are you that hungry?"

"If a fellow catches a lake monster," Jean-Paul said, "folks will listen to what he has to say."

"The way you talk," Andre said, "you better catch two lake monsters."

Jean-Paul clambered into his old fishing boat and rowed those giant fishing lures back and forth across Lake Utopia without catching so much as a nibble.

"There's nothing out here," Jean-Paul decided. "I've been fishing for fool's gold."

Just then Old Ned broke through the water, all teeth and roar with fangs as large as pirate cutlasses. He chewed down onto Jean-Paul's homemade jumbo fishing lure and got his left rear molar snagged in one of the hooks.

Jean-Paul threw his net and tangled it around Old Ned's big, wet, smelly, shaggy hide, catching him fast.

"Now I got you, Old Ned," Jean-Paul said.

Old Ned just lay helpless in Jean-Paul's net. Jean-Paul was struck by the look of the lake monster's eyes, all big and flat and wet like beach stone. Old Ned lay there, still and calm, staring up at Jean-Paul and weeping bucket-sized tears.

"Why, you're no monster," Jean-Paul said, reaching out to cut the beast free. Jean-Paul waved as the lake monster dove down into the murky depths.

Every three or four years Old Ned is seen again, as regular as the change of the seasons. He is usually spotted when the logs are in the river—some say he is looking and listening for his old friend, Jean-Paul, and one more taste of salt cod and pickled pork.

LOCATION: Old Ned lives in Lake Utopia, about one kilometre north of the town of St. George, New Brunswick.

DIET: Otters and eels and beavers and trout

SIZE: He's thirty to fifty feet long, and about as heavy as a transport truck.

DESCRIPTION: Old Ned is a huge eel-like beast with a head as large as a bathtub, teeth as long and sharp as swords, and a shaggy hide like a buffalo's.

FREQUENCY OF SIGHTINGS: Old Ned is seen every few years. He was first spotted way back in the 1870s by a lumberjack crew, while they were harvesting floating logs.

SPECIAL MONSTER-HUNTING ADVICE: Old Ned is kind of shy, and almost gentle compared to most lake monsters. He has a bit of a sweet tooth, so a bucket of molasses might go a long way towards bringing him up to the surface—and I've heard that he's fond of the taste of salt cod and pickled pork.

CRESSIE (NEWFOUNDLAND)

"The water out in that lake is nearly a quarter of a kilometre deep in spots," Esau Dalton said. "What goes down there don't come back up too soon."

"Listen to you talk," Donnie Parrot said. "I can tell you're lying on account of your lips are moving."

"It's no lie," Esau said. "I've been out there. You drop a fishing line in and there's no telling what might take hold of your bait. Might be Cressie herself, or one of her young."

Donnie tapped the side of his head and rolled his eyes, but Esau paid no attention.

"There are swarms of eels swimming through those waters," Esau said, "and they come in all sizes. Back in the early 1950s I thought I seen an overturned dory floating on the water, but when I came up on it, it dove down."

"The dory dove?" Donnie asked. "Are you sure you weren't looking at a submarine?"

"It weren't no dory nor no submarine," Esau said. "It were Cressie herself, as big as life. *Wooden howoot*, the Mi'kmaq call her. Pond devil, a giant eel that stretches longer than two dories put together—at least twenty feet and maybe more."

"Sounds more like hogwash than howoot," Donnie said with a snort.

"No sir, no hogwash at all. It were the same as old Grandmother Anthony saw when she was but a girl out picking berries. That was a long time back and that pond devil is out there still."

"You're talking foolishness, man."

"I'm talking fact," Esau said. "Not more than twenty years ago I seen three Mountie divers coming out of that lake after a bush plane had gone down into it. They swore they'd been set on by giant eels, some as thick as a man's right thigh, that pretty near chewed them to pieces."

"Eels grow big," Donnie said with a shrug of his shoulders.

"Certain tooting," Esau agreed. "But how big? Now that's the sixty-four-thousand-dollar question, isn't it? I have a sneaking suspicion those eels were nothing more than hungry babies getting set to grow."

Donnie thought on that and shivered. "It's getting cold," Donnie said, only the sun was as warm as a Saturday night bath.

LOCATION: On the northeast coast of Newfoundland, about twenty kilometres east of Springdale, is the little town of Robert's Arm. It is here that you'll find Crescent Lake, where Cressie lives.

DIET: Cressie seems fond of the taste of wetsuits and divers' flippers.

SIZE: Twenty feet long

DESCRIPTION: Cressie is a long, eel-like monster with a flat, fish-like head; she looks something like a sturgeon, stretching out and wiggling. She's got a big old mouth and according to all reports, she sure likes to eat.

FREQUENCY OF SIGHTINGS: At least every couple of years there's a brand-new Cressie sighting. It is believed that a whole colony of these giant eel-like creatures lives in Crescent Lake.

SPECIAL MONSTER-HUNTING ADVICE: I don't recommend diving.

THE HIDEY-HINDER
(NOVA SCOTIA)

More years ago than you have fingers or toes, Rufus Carboy followed close behind young Allan into the heart of Dagger Woods with mischief on his mind. Young Allan's sweetheart was Janine—one of the prettiest girls in Antigonish.

"I'll sneak up and scare Allan away," Rufus decided. "If he runs far enough then I'll be free to court Janine and he will be no more trouble for me."

Now folks who knew better steered clear of Dagger Woods. Hadn't little Saundra nearly been grabbed by the Hidey-Hinder a few years ago while she was picking blueberries?

Young Allan wasn't thinking too clearly because his heart was in his eyes. He was thinking about the bouquet of wildflowers he'd pick for sweet Janine. He didn't hear old Rufus sneaking up behind him, not until it was too late.

"Booga-wooga-booga!" Rufus shouted, trying to scare young Allan as he stooped to pick a devil's paintbrush.

"BOOGA-OOGA-WOOGLY-BOOGA!!!" shouted a voice that sounded like a cross between a roll of summer thunder and a long grape-soda burp from directly behind Rufus's back.

Rufus didn't stop to look. He ran like his feet were lit up by lightning bolts.

Allan stood up and turned to see the Hidey-Hinder, there in bold daylight, staring back at him.

What did it look like?

Allan won't tell you. He hasn't said a word since he stumbled out of Dagger Woods, his hair bleached white as snow, his eyes as wild as blackberries.

"Boogaboogaboogaboogabooga," is all that he'll say, wiggling his fingers across his lips the whole day long. "Boogaboogaboogabooga."

Folks who know their elbow from their boogabooga stay far away from Dagger Woods.

LOCATION: About twenty kilometres east of Antigonish, Nova Scotia—or directly behind you

DIET: Whatever it can sneak up on

SIZE: Just as big as it has to be

DESCRIPTION: The Hidey-Hinder has long, stick-like grabby-fingers that reach for you, and if you turn around fast enough you will see—ARRRRRGHHHHH! boogabooga-boogabooga…

FREQUENCY OF SIGHTINGS: Nobody will say how often it's been seen.

SPECIAL MONSTER-HUNTING ADVICE: The Hidey-Hinder sneaks up on unsuspecting folks in the wilderness. If you hear it coming you'll want to jump as quick as you can to catch a look at it. That's the only way to scare it off. But you better have pogo sticks for feet, because that old Hidey-Hinder is as fast as a cricket.

THE SELKIE (NOVA SCOTIA)

Mariah stood on the shore, staring at the roaring ocean waters. It had been seven years since the purple-haired pirates had kidnapped her from her home in Scotland and sailed her to the shores of Cape Breton.

"If I could only swim back home to Scotland I would be happy," she said. "I wish I were a big, fast-moving fish."

She stepped out into the water, feeling the waves lap at her ankles. She stepped a little farther and the seawater tickled her knees.

"I miss Mom and Dad," she said, weeping seven slow, salty tears into the pounding surf.

Seven and only seven.

Seven is magic, don't you know? There were seven dwarves and seven ravens and there are seven stars in the Big Dipper and seven days in a week. As the seventh tear splashed down and mingled with the waves, a great grey seal rose up out of the water and stood there, staring at Mariah. The seal's skin fell away and Mariah gasped in amazement.

There standing before her was a selkie, a seal-man. Mariah had heard of such things from her grandmother. She'd told Mariah that seal-men were not to be trusted, but this one's eyes looked soft and kind.

"I am the prince of the seal-people," the selkie said. "I have tasted the sorrow swimming in your seven tears and it has touched my heart in seven different ways."

The seal-prince tore his skin in two and placed half of it about Mariah's shoulders. In seven beats of her heart she became a grey seal.

"Now we can swim for home," the seal-prince said, placing the second half of the skin about his own shoulders and changing back into a seal.

"Perhaps I am home already," the Mariah-selkie replied.

In the evening the purple-haired pirates followed Mariah's tracks down to the water's edge, but they could see no sign of her. They stood on the shore and scratched their purple heads—but Mariah, who is now called the Selkie-Queen of the Seven Seas, only returns to the Cape Breton shoreline to laugh and play in the waves of the sea.

LOCATION: Since the early 1800s, selkies have been reported off the coast of Cape Breton.

DIET: They eat kelp and small fish.

SIZE: In seal form, a selkie can grow to at least ten feet long and over seven hundred pounds.

DESCRIPTION: In their human form, selkies appear much like you or me, but both male and female selkies have been described as unusually beautiful.

FREQUENCY OF SIGHTINGS: It is hard to figure how often selkies are seen, because they spend most of their life in seal form.

SPECIAL MONSTER-HUNTING ADVICE: It is bad luck to catch a selkie. The sea may grow angry at a fisherman that catches one. Keeping a selkie captive may bring bad weather.

THE MERMAID (NEWFOUNDLAND)

Seashells are the cellphones of the sea.

If you find a seashell as pink as the big toe of a baby angel and as small as the cup of your mother's hand and hold it to your ear, you will hear the sound of mermaids singing to the rain clouds. No one can tell you exactly which shell to pick up and listen to, but when you find it you will know.

Mermaids have been seen dozens of times in the waters surrounding the Maritimes and the stories about them run as thick as blackflies in the north woods.

This is one of them.

In 1912 a mermaid tried to climb aboard the dory of a Newfoundland fisherman named Ringo Tattingo.

"She was nearly as long as my dory," Ringo Tattingo swore, "and as pretty as you can imagine from her belly button on up. But below there was nothing but fish tail. Her hair was long and wavy with streaks of blue—the colour of the sky reflected in the sea."

Ringo Tattingo swung his oars at the mermaid just as hard as he could.

"My great-grandfather, Mingo Tattingo, saw the same mermaid when he was a boy," Ringo Tattingo said. "He said she promised she'd come back and carry him off and let him see what the clouds looked like from under the sea—and I do believe she thought I was him."

Ringo Tattingo looked thoughtful then.

"I wonder if she was a fish that was part woman or a woman that was part fish," Ringo Tattingo said. "But fish or woman, I wasn't about to let her on board my dory. The clouds look fine to me from this side up, thank you very kindly."

But once a week old Ringo Tattingo still rows on out to the St. John's Narrows with a big box of chocolates and a bouquet of forget-me-nots that he scatters over the lonesome blue-streaked waves.

And every night you will find old Ringo Tattingo squatting on the end of a St. John's dock with a seashell, as pink as the big toe of a baby angel, pressed tightly to his right ear.

LOCATION: St. John's Harbour, Newfoundland

DIET: Dreams, wishes, and frosted cupcakes

SIZE: The mermaid that Ringo Tattingo saw was nearly twelve feet long, from the tip of her nose to the farthest fin of her tail; however, mermaids range in size from as small as a thimble to as big as a whale.

DESCRIPTION: It is said that mermaids are even more beautiful than selkies, but don't ever tell a selkie that.

FREQUENCY OF SIGHTINGS: There are as many mermaids as there are waves on the sea. Count them if you don't believe me.

SPECIAL MONSTER-HUNTING ADVICE: Bait a candy-cane hook with marmalade and marzipan if you want to catch a mermaid, but make sure you have a fish tank big enough to hold her. A mermaid will leave a nasty ring in your bathtub, if you keep her there for too long.

THE COLEMAN FROG (NEW BRUNSWICK)

Old Fred Coleman was a lonely old man. So lonely that he made a pet out of a bullfrog, which he named Ribber.

Bread and beer and buttermilk every morning, that's what old Fred Coleman fed his bullfrog, Ribber. Oh sure, some folks would give a frog fistfuls of beetles and moths and grasshoppers, but Fred's long-sticky-tongued pond hopper thrived on people food. That might be the reason the bullfrog grew so darned large that it had to be stopped before it drank Fredericton dry of buttermilk.

Two of the town's bravest young men went down to Killarney Lake and dynamited the mud hole where the Godzilla of bullfrogs was hunkered down. The blast blew the bullfrog clear out of the mudhole. The frog didn't survive the explosion, but enough of the frog was left behind for old Fred to have it stuffed and mounted.

So now the frog—the largest in the world—sits on display in Fredericton's York-Sunbury Museum. It's squatting in a showcase, but if you lean close enough and give a big old bullfrog-sized sniff I'll bet you can still smell the yeasty reek of Fred's home-baked bread and home-brewed beer, not to mention the nostril-curdling funk of two-hundred-year-old buttermilk.

It's enough to make you croak.

LOCATION: Fredericton, New Brunswick

DIET: Beer, bread, and buttermilk

SIZE: Stretched out, the Coleman Frog measures nearly five feet from front foot to back leg, and weighs in at a sturdy forty pounds.

DESCRIPTION: He's big and green and mottled.

FREQUENCY OF SIGHTINGS: There's only one and you can see it every day the museum is open.

SPECIAL MONSTER-HUNTING ADVICE: There's not an awful lot I can tell you about catching this frog, since he isn't going anywhere these days.

THE PARKER ROAD PHANTOM (NOVA SCOTIA)

"**G**et up on my shoulders," Dan said.

It was a tricky clamber for little Patrick, climbing up onto his big brother Dan's back while wearing Granddad's old army overcoat. The overcoat smelled funny—it had been hanging in their grandparents' attic for at least twenty years and on Granddad's own back for nearly twenty more before that.

Truth be told, there wasn't a sniffle's worth of difference between the mouldy smell of that attic and the foul tobacco-and-beef-jerky odour of old Granddad at his worst—or even his best.

"I can't breathe," little Patrick said. "I need to take this stocking off my face. It smells funny."

"*You* smell funny," Dan said. "Those nylons are nearly brand new. They've only been worn the once and you better be careful with them. I have to have them back in Grand-Auntie Terrilee's dresser drawer by tomorrow, before she knows they're missing."

It was April of 1969 and Dan and Patrick had decided to play a trick on their grandparents. Patrick perched on Dan's shoulders as they prowled around the yard, disguised by their Grand-dad's old army jacket and the thick Nova Scotian fog.

But a few other folks spotted the lumbering two-kid figure and decided that the Parker Road Phantom—a Bigfoot-like beast who had stomped around these woods back in the early 1800s—had returned.

For nights afterward, cars parked up and down Parker Road, looking for a sign of the ghostly giant. It wasn't until 2008 that the boys finally came clean and confessed their escapade.

I have changed the names for the sake of privacy, but the story is true.

Nevertheless, folks in the area still wonder whether the hulking shape in the fog that was seen that night was actually a Nova Scotian sasquatch.

LOCATION: Berwick, Nova Scotia

DIET: Whatever it can catch

SIZE: Some say the beast stood a good twenty feet tall, but if you calculate the height of your little brother standing on top of your big brother's shoulders, you'll probably figure it was nine feet or so.

DESCRIPTION: The Parker Road Phantom has a big, baggy shape, and it is able to run extremely fast.

FREQUENCY OF SIGHTINGS: It was seen back in the 1800s and then seen again in April 1969.

SPECIAL MONSTER-HUNTING ADVICE: The phantom seems to like foggy nights best, so I recommend bringing your fog lights with you.

OLD SHUCK (NOVA SCOTIA)

One late October evening, when the moon was staring wide and full and the stars were peeking and gleaming from the heavens, Willy Wallace went out hunting rabbits in the Cape Breton woods with a few of his friends.

It was just a little past midnight and a long way to dawn when a horrible howling was heard just ahead of the hunters. The hunters' hounds turned and galloped for home, yipping and yelping like a pack of spanked puppies.

"That's Old Shuck," Willy's best friend, Amos, told him. "An old black dog as big as a full-grown bear. He hunts the night for lost souls, and if you see him bad luck is sure to follow. He's what they call a forerunner. When he comes we'd all better go."

Willy raised his musket and grinned fiercely.

"He better hope he can outrun a musket ball," Willy said. "If he thinks he can spoil my rabbit hunt, he's got another think coming."

"He's bad luck, Willy," Amos warned. "He'll strike you down just as sure as apples fall from trees."

"I'll sew his hide into fur hunting socks," Willy said.

At that Old Shuck stepped out of the woods. He was as black as a hockey puck, with eyes that glowed like headlights, teeth as long and sharp as midwinter icicles, and a head as big as a boxcar.

BANG!

Willy fired.

Old Shuck snapped at Willy, tearing the musket from the stubborn man's grip and chomping it up like it was nothing but a big chew toy.

Willy turned and ran. He galloped right out of his hunting boots, passed the hounds, and wore his big woolly hunting socks down to nothing but a thin strand of dirty grey thread tailing behind him as he knocked over trees and plowed straight through the hillsides as he went.

The long, rambling trail he cleared as he ran eventually became known as the Cabot Trail.

LOCATION: Deathbeds, wakes, and fire hydrants—Old Shuck is usually seen around Cape Breton and anywhere the Celtic roots grow strong and deep.

DIET: Old bones and muskets and the occasional chew toy

SIZE: Old Shuck can stand as big as he needs to. When he growls and raises his hackles, he gets a little larger.

DESCRIPTION: As black as a grease-stained hockey puck, Old Shuck is like a giant pit bull that swallows other pit bulls whole. His growl sounds like something you might hear in the wrong end of a grizzly-bear stomach and his eyes shine like fog lamps in the night.

FREQUENCY OF SIGHTINGS: Old Shuck has been prowling the hills since Scots started wearing kilts.

SPECIAL MONSTER-HUNTING ADVICE: Talk to your local dogcatcher.

AN ACADIAN WEREWOLF (NEW BRUNSWICK)

Marie Cormier was a pretty Acadian girl who lived by the Miramichi River with her father, lumberjack Felix Cormier.

One early September morning a man rapped on their door with three hard knocks. BANG – BANG – BANG!

Marie opened the door. Standing there was a lean, tall man wearing a long grey cloak. His eyes seemed to shine like a pair of full moons.

"My name is Joe Boudreau," he said. "I live in the far valley. Your daddy is poor but I am not. If you marry me, girl, I will see that he has all the money he needs and I will treat you well."

Marie talked to her father and he told her to follow her heart.

"My heart tells me to take care of my daddy," Marie said, "so I will marry this Joe Boudreau. He seems like a kind man and I am certain he will take care of me."

Marie was not wrong. Joe Boudreau saw that both Marie and her father had everything they needed. However, on their wedding night Boudreau gave his bride a very strange gift—a blunderbuss pistol, and a bag of silver shot.

"Keep the pistol with you wherever you go," Joe Boudreau told her. "Especially on nights when the moon is full."

For ten years Marie and Boudreau lived happily. They had an easy life, except that every full moon, Boudreau would walk into the woods and not come out until the morning. One night Marie followed him, taking care to carry the pistol and silver shot he had given her.

She caught up to him at the foot of the old hill. There, beneath the light of the full moon, he pulled his skin off—and, turning it inside out, he changed into a wolf. He was a *loup-garou* (that's what Acadians call a werewolf). His body seemed to stretch and creak like a pine tree blowing in the midnight breeze as his limbs lengthened and his claws grew out. His face wolfed forward until it looked like he was wearing a German Shepherd on his head.

The werewolf charged at Marie and she pulled the trigger of the pistol and blasted him full of silver shot. When the smoke cleared, Boudreau was lying in the dirt.

"You've been a good wife for ten years, until you shot me," Boudreau said. "I leave everything to you."

And then he howled once, like a lonely old wolf, and closed his eyes.

Later that year Marie gave birth to a daughter with long grey hair and eyes that shone like full moons. She called the little girl Luna and loved her with all of her heart, yet on every full moon Marie kept a very close watch.

LOCATION: Miramichi, New Brunswick

DIET: Rabbits, sheep, and goats

SIZE: A full-grown werewolf, or *loup-garou*, stands nearly eight feet tall.

DESCRIPTION: A *loup-garou* wears the skin of a wolf, and looks like a large, hairy German shepherd standing on its hind legs.

FREQUENCY OF SIGHTINGS: Every full moon, or so the old legends say

SPECIAL MONSTER-HUNTING ADVICE: Never leave home without a silver bullet.

SHEILA THE SEA HAG (PRINCE EDWARD ISLAND)

Sheila the Sea Hag lives on the bottom of Bedeque Bay, just outside of Summerside, in a secret cave beneath a secret island. Some say she looks like a beautiful woman, with hair that streams down past her shoulders and eyes as deep as the ocean's heart. Some say she looks like a hideous sea monster, with a nose that grows right into her chin and ears that droop and dangle like rubber tire swings.

Some folks say she looks like my Great Aunt Murgatroyde Hermione Legoosh, but I really wouldn't go that far.

Some folks will tell you that it is her breathing that stirs the waters of the Northumberland Strait. Sheila inhales—whooooosh—and the tide rolls in. Then Sheila exhales—whooooosh—and the tide runs out.

And when she snores???

A tidal wave!

If you have trouble sleeping, many of the old people will swear it's because Sheila the Sea Hag has crawled up out of the water and stolen your breath to feed her own.

Which isn't true.

Sheila far prefers Prince Edward Island french fries—with salt and vinegar and a whole lot of ketchup. Tastes a whole lot better than sleep-breath, you bet for sure.

LOCATION: Bedeque Bay, Prince Edward Island, in a sea cave beneath a tiny island

DIET: French-fried potatoes

SIZE: Either human-sized or nearly twenty feet long, depending on who you are talking to. Some believe that Sheila the Sea Hag can change her size depending on the flow of the tide.

DESCRIPTION: At her ugliest, Sheila the Sea Hag looks like an old woman with the tail of a sea worm instead of legs. At her prettiest, she looks a lot like your mother.

FREQUENCY OF SIGHTINGS: Like the werewolf, Sheila gets grumpy on full-moon nights.

SPECIAL MONSTER-HUNTING ADVICE: Whatever you do, don't forget the ketchup.

THE CAPE SPLIT KELPIE (NOVA SCOTIA)

If you see a kelpie from a distance it will look like a large, dark horse the colour of thick sea mud. Get a little closer and you might notice a tinge of slimy green on its hide. Get closer yet, and you will see the frill of gills hidden behind the kelpie's ears. Get too close and you might wish you hadn't.

A kelpie lures its victims closer by pretending to be a lost horse. Everyone who sees a kelpie feels the urge to climb on board—but if you mount it you will find yourself stuck fast. Kelpies are made of something stickier than the gooiest of glues—all soft and oozy, like melting black licorice.

Once you're stuck the kelpie will gallop out into the pounding surf and drag you down under the waves, where it will feed your flesh to its herd of man-eating seahorses and throw your bones to the dogfish to gnaw on. Some old legends say that the kelpie will leave behind nothing but your liver, floating like a cork on the incoming tide.

I guess nobody except Great-Uncle Wilfred von Teaselhauffer likes to eat liver, and he smells funny on the best of days.

The only way to protect yourself from a kelpie is to scrub your hands with soap all over. The kelpie does not like the taste of soap, and if you're all soapy you'll slide free from its sticky hide. The kelpie also doesn't like the sound of cheery singing, particularly the "Happy Birthday" song. Singing "Happy Birthday" twice while washing your hands will make you doubly safe.

The old folks who live around Cape Split will tell you of a phantom horse who can be heard galloping madly towards the cliff, splashing and crashing in the pounding waves below. Some storytellers believe this phantom horse is an invisible kelpie.

I don't know about you, but I don't plan on getting close enough to that sticky old horse to find out for sure.

LOCATION: Cape Split, Nova Scotia

DIET: Unwary riders and beach grass

SIZE: A kelpie is the size of a large horse or a small pony, depending on whether the wicked old beast is trying to lure grown-ups or children.

DESCRIPTION: It looks like a horse until you get close enough to spot the gills that frill up behind its ears.

FREQUENCY OF SIGHTINGS: A kelpie will rise up from the low-tide mud and gallop out when the Fundy tide comes roaring in.

SPECIAL MONSTER-HUNTING ADVICE: Kelpies are afraid of dogs, particularly farm dogs. Some say that a farm dog can be used to herd kelpies. Other folks will tell you that a kelpie will gallop off at the sight of a dog—faster than a storyteller after his last story is told and done.

DEDICATION

I want to dedicate this picture book to the little Maritime monster I told stories to every night before bedtime—my daughter, Sarah Skye, who put the stars in the heavens and taught them how to smile.

—Steve Vernon

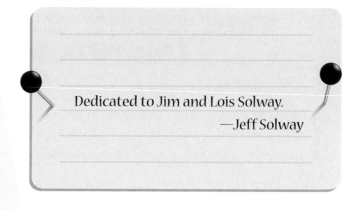

Dedicated to Jim and Lois Solway.

—Jeff Solway

Nimbus Publishing Limited
PO Box 9166, Halifax, NS B3K 5M8
(902) 455-4286 www.nimbus.ca

Printed and bound in Canada

Library and Archives Canada Cataloguing in Publication

Vernon, Steve
Maritime monsters : a field guide / Steve Vernon ; illustrations by Jeff Solway.
ISBN 978-1-55109-727-5

1. Monsters—Atlantic Provinces—Humor—Juvenile literature. I. Solway, Jeff II. Title.

QL89.V47 2009   j398.209715'0454   C2009-902863-8

We acknowledge the financial support of the Government of Canada through the Book Publishing Industry Development Program (BPIDP) and the Canada Council, and of the Province of Nova Scotia through the Department of Tourism, Culture and Heritage for our publishing activities.